Pooh ☑ P9-CBD-062

A Tigger Inside and Out

MOUSE WORKS

It was a wonderful morning to be a Tigger!
The rain had stopped, and lots of nice, big puddles
were just waiting to be splashed in all over the
Hundred-Acre Wood.

Tigger bounced and splashed in every one,
covering himself in mud from head to toe.

Suddenly Pooh, Rabbit, and Piglet jumped out
from behind some bushes.

"A clean Tigger is a happy Tigger," said Rabbit as they popped Tigger in a tub of sudsy water.

"And a happy Tigger is a clean Tigger," added Pooh as he grabbed a scrub brush and some soap and went to work.

"He doesn't look very happy to me," said Piglet.

When his bath was over, and Tigger
stepped out of the tub, his friends just stared.

"Who are you?" asked Piglet.

"I'm Tigger!" said Tigger. "Who else
would I be?"

"But you can't be Tigger.
He has stripes," said Pooh.
    Tigger looked down at himself.
His stripes were gone!

"He has two ears and a tail like I do," said Rabbit. "Maybe he's a rabbit."

"Hey, yeah!" said Tigger. "And I can jump, too. I must be a rabbit."

And so Tigger and Rabbit went off to do some gardening.

Tigger was a terrible gardener. Instead of pro-
tecting Rabbit's garden from bugs, he let the bugs
get fat and happy eating all of Rabbit's tomatoes.
   "You're not a rabbit!" yelled Rabbit, chasing
Tigger into the woods. "And you never will be!"

If I'm not a rabbit, what am I? wondered
Tigger. Then he saw Pooh and got an idea.
"Hey, Buddy Bear, wait up!" he called to his
friend. "I think I'm a bear!"

"Well, it's time for us bears to have some unch," said Pooh, as he led Tigger to a beehive.

"Go ahead!" Pooh said. "I'm right behind ou!" But instead of using the ladder, Tigger ounced up on his tail, accidentally knocking the eehive to the ground. Pooh watched a swarm of ngry bees chase his friend away.

"Oh, bother," said Pooh. "He's definitely not bear."

Pooh followed Tigger and found him moping
under a tree. "Cheer up," said Pooh, "maybe
you're a Piglet."

So Tigger and Pooh went to Piglet's house to find out.

Tigger tried to put on one of Piglet's shirts, but it was much too small for him.

"I guess I'm not a Piglet, either," said Tigger sadly.

Tigger seemed so unhappy that Pooh and Piglet decided there was only one way to help. They would paint Tigger's stripes back on so he could be a Tigger again.

When they were finished, Tigger felt like his old self.

"I'm a Tigger!" he shouted as he bounced out the door. "I'm a Tigger!"

Just then thunder echoed through the Hundred-Acre Wood. Within minutes, a spring shower washed away Tigger's wonderful new stripes.

"I'm not a Tigger! I'm not a Tigger!" moaned Tigger, feeling more miserable than ever.

Just then Eeyore walked by. "Hello, Tigger,"
he said.

"Hey, you just called me Tigger!" said Tigger.

"Well, why not? You *are* Tigger, aren't you?" Eeyore asked.

"No," answered Tigger. "I don't have any stripes."

"Aw, that's all right," Eeyore said. "It's what's *inside* you that makes you a Tigger, not what's *outside*. You'll always be Tigger to me."

"Hoo, hoo, hoo! I'm a Tigger, after all!" shouted Tigger, bouncing and bouncing on the end of his tail.

Suddenly, he heard a loud POP! — and a stripe appeared!

He bounced some more — POP! POP! POP!—
and with every bounce, a new stripe appeared.
Soon he had every last stripe that had washed off
in the tub!

Tigger bounced off into the sunset, happy as a Tigger with stripes should be. As he bounced, he sang this little song:

I'm a Tigger without a doubt.
A real live Tigger, inside and out!